What Do You Like?

What

Michael Grejniec

Do You Like?

North-South Books   New York

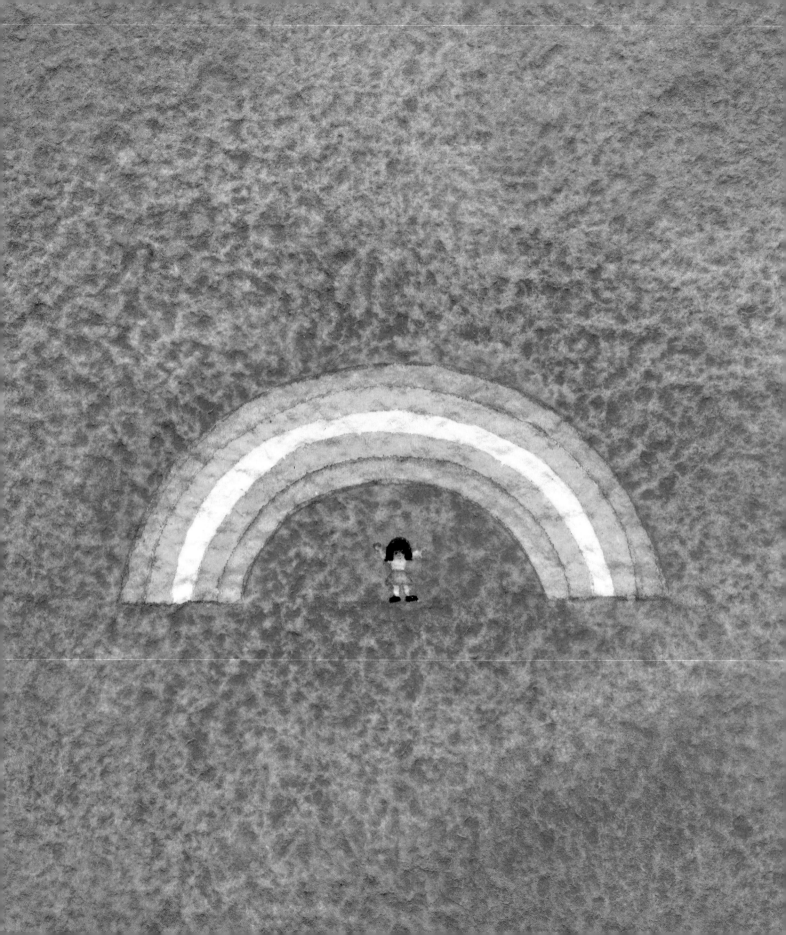

I like the rainbow.

I like the rainbow, too.

I like to play.

I like to play, too.

I like my cat.

I like my cat, too.

I like fruit.

I like fruit, too.

I like music.

I like music, too.

I like to fly.

I like to fly, too.

I love my mother.
I love my mother, too.

What do you like?
What do you love?

Published in the United States by North-South Books Inc., New York.

Published simultaneously in Great Britain, Canada,
Australia and New Zealand in 1992 by North-South Books,
an imprint of Nord-Süd Verlag AG, Gossau Zürich, Switzerland.

Library of Congress Cataloging-in-Publication Data
Grejniec, Michael.
What Do You Like? / Michael Grejniec.
Summary: Children discover that they can like
the same things and still be different.
ISBN 1-55858-175-8 (trade binding)
ISBN 1-55858-176-6 (library binding)
[1. Individuality—Fiction.] I. Title.
PZ7.G8625Wg 1992
[E]—dc20 92-3481

A CIP catalogue record for this book
is available from The British Library

1 3 5 7 9 10 8 6 4 2
Printed in Belgium

The art was painted with Pelican and Windsor Newton
watercolors on Colombe paper. The color separations were made
from transparencies, rather than the original art, so that the texture of the
watercolor paper would appear in the printed book. All the images were
greatly enlarged, to accentuate the details and the rough edges of
the painting. The interior images are 250% larger than
the originals. The cover art is 400% larger.

Book design and hand lettering
by Michael Grejniec